W9-ASL-470

CPS-MORRILL SCHOOL LIBRARY

3 4880 05000695 1   E WIL
The best winds

DATE DUE

E
WIL

3 4880 05000695 1
Williams, Laura E.

The best winds

CPS-MORRILL SCHOOL LIBRARY
CHICAGO PUBLIC SCHOOLS
6011 S ROCKWELL ST
CHICAGO, IL 60629

778392 01186   34971C   0001

The Best Winds

Laura E. Williams

Illustrated by
Eujin Kim Neilan

BOYDS MILLS PRESS

The author wishes to thank John Barresi, publisher, kitelife.com

Text copyright © 2006 by Laura E. Williams
Illustrations copyright © 2006 by Eujin Kim Neilan
All rights reserved

Published by Boyds Mills Press, Inc.
A Highlights Company
815 Church Street
Honesdale, Pennsylvania 18431
Printed in China

CIP data is available

First edition, 2006
The text of this book is set in 15-point Minion.
The illustrations are done in acrylic.

Visit our Web site at www.boydsmillspress.com

10 9 8 7 6 5 4 3 2 1

For grandfathers and their stories, and for Tamara Visco, who got me back to Korea
— L. E. W.

For my son, Paul
— E. K. N.

Grandfather moved in after Grandmother died. The old man wore
hanboks and wouldn't wear his shoes inside the house.

Jinho and his friends laughed at his ancient ways. They said his hanboks looked like bathrobes.

One evening, Grandfather said to his grandson, "Tonight I will show you how to make a kite, for the best winds will be here soon." Jinho wanted to go outside to skateboard, but his mother nudged him toward the kitchen table instead. The boy sighed and sat down beside his grandfather. Grandfather held a large, faded kite in place with fingers as stiff as bamboo while Jinho traced it onto new white paper.

Grandfather said, "There's nothing like flying a *bangpae-yeon*, a shield kite. Why, I remember when I was a boy and my grandfather taught me . . ." Jinho rolled his eyes and stopped listening to his grandfather's story. He was tired of those tales from long, long ago — tales about fishing, tales about growing up in a small village by the sea, tales about boring things.

After Jinho traced the kite, he cut the paper and threw away the scraps. By the time they were done, it was too dark to go skateboarding. It was time to go to bed.

The following night, Grandfather said, "Now we will paint the kite, because the best winds will be here soon."

Jinho looked at his father, hoping he'd let him play video games, but he pointed toward the kitchen table. Jinho scowled. He didn't want to make a kite. Nobody made kites anymore. They bought them at the toy store, and hardly anyone flew them.

Grandfather finished mixing the dyes with hands as wrinkled as old rice paper. Leaning back, he said, "When I was a boy, just your age, Jinho, my grandfather showed me . . ."

Again Jinho stopped listening. He dipped the brush into the bright colors and swirled them onto the kite paper. After a while, he smiled. This wasn't as fun as video games or skateboarding, but it was OK. Grandfather's voice chirped on and on like a cricket in the background.

The next night, Grandfather said, "Now we will make the frame."

"I know," Jinho said quickly. "We must hurry, because the best winds will be here soon."

Grandfather stared at Jinho for a long, quiet moment. Jinho suddenly wished he hadn't interrupted. Then Grandfather nodded slowly and held the kite frame, but his hands quivered like the leaves on the ginkgo tree. And he said, "Long ago, when my grandfather helped me . . ."

Jinho didn't pay any attention to his grandfather's story as he concentrated on tying the bamboo sticks together and attaching the paper. Finally it was finished.

"Now we make the tails," Grandfather said, opening a small sack of silk scarves.
"The tails give the kite stability and dignity."

With hands as pale as fish bellies, Jinho's grandfather handed over the scarves, one by one. The boy carefully tied them to the kite.

Just then, Grandfather tilted his head to one side. "Listen," he said. "The best winds are coming."

The boy listened, but he didn't hear anything different.

Grandfather said, "I remember when I first heard the best winds. My grandfather, that would be your great-great-grandfather, Jinho . . ."

Jinho ignored his grandfather and held up the finished kite. It was tall and it was broad. It was bright and it was light. The tails fluttered across the kitchen floor. Jinho had to admit it was more beautiful than any kite he had ever seen in the toy store. Suddenly, he pictured himself flying this magnificent kite with all his friends watching. He couldn't wait until the next morning.

That night Jinho barely slept. At last the sun glowed pink through the cloudy sky, and the boy raced into the kitchen and grabbed the kite. Then he dashed outside and called to his friends as he ran to the park.

A sudden gust of wind pulled the kite out of Jinho's hands. It swerved and jerked about in the sky, the tails snapping back and forth like angry snakes. The boy desperately tried to steady it, but his clumsy hands tangled in the string. What had Grandfather told him about flying a kite? All he heard was the soft chirp of a cricket in his head.

With a last shudder, the kite flipped over and crashed through the branches of a tree, then it fell to the sidewalk like an injured bird.

Jinho ran and picked up the kite. It had a big, ugly tear in it. With a heavy heart, the boy slowly walked home.

Grandfather stood on the porch, his eyes gleaming with tears. "You couldn't wait for the best winds?" he asked. "You couldn't wait for me?"

"I'm so sorry, Grandfather."

Jinho took the ruined kite into his room. Sitting on his bed, he emptied his bank. Two dollars and seventeen cents — that wasn't even enough to buy a cheap kite, never mind a beautiful one. He ran his hands along the frame of the kite. It still held strong. In a flash, he knew what he had to do.

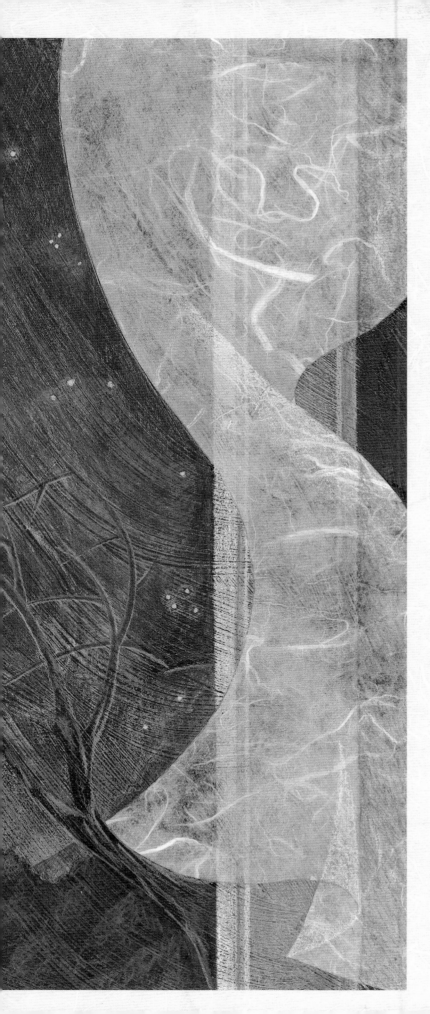

After dinner that evening, Grandfather cupped his hand like a seashell to his ear. "Listen," he said sadly. "The best winds are nearly here. They will arrive with the rising sun, but we have no kite to greet them."

Jinho listened carefully. He thought he heard a slight change in the wind blowing through the trees.

The next morning, Jinho awoke early. He raced into Grandfather's room. "Wake up," Jinho shouted. "We must hurry, or we'll miss the best winds."

Grandfather slowly opened his eyes. When he saw the new kite, he smiled.

"It's not as beautiful as the first one," Jinho apologized.

Grandfather pulled the boy into his arms. "It's not beauty that makes a kite good and true. It's the care and love that go into making it. And I have a feeling this kite is far finer than the first one."

The old man got out of bed and dressed in his best hanbok.

As the two walked to the park, Jinho's friends followed along.

Jinho flicked the tails of the kite with pride.

When they reached the park, Grandfather said, "I'll hold the kite, and you run with the line."

Jinho nodded. He ran. The wind caught the kite and lifted it high . . . higher . . . almost to the clouds. Suddenly the kite plummeted. It swerved and jumped. It dived and swirled.

Grandfather shouted, but Jinho couldn't hear the words. Then two hands as strong as mountains covered the boy's. Standing behind him, Grandfather pulled the string in, trying to steady the kite.

For a moment the kite trembled as though it would come crashing down to earth, but then it soared higher in a graceful arc, the tails streaming out. The line pulled tight. "You did it!" Jinho shouted.

"*We* did it," Grandfather said, letting go.

Jinho laughed. He loved the string tugging in his hands, almost as though the kite wanted to break free and fly away.

"Was it like this when you and Great-Great-Grandfather flew your first kite?" Jinho asked.

Grandfather laid a hand, warm as love, on the boy's shoulder. "Just like this," he agreed. Then he told the story of long, long ago, and Jinho listened.